SHONEN JUMP'S

Yu-Gi-Oh! GX

NIGHT SPIES

SHONEN JUMP'S

Yu-Gi-Oh! GX

NIGHT SPIES

Adapted by Tracey West

SCHOLASTIC INC.
New York Toronto London Auckland Sydney
Mexico City New Delhi Hong Kong Buenos Aires

ISBN-13: 978-0-439-88832-5
ISBN-10: 0-439-88832-8

Published by Scholastic Inc.
SCHOLASTIC and associated logos are trademarks and/or registered
trademarks of Scholastic Inc.

12 11 10 9 8 7 6 5 4 3 2 1   7 8 9 10 11 12/0

Designed by Phil Falco
Printed in the U.S.A.
First printing, January 2007

SHONEN JUMP'S

Yu-Gi-Oh! GX

NIGHT SPIES

• CHAPTER ONE •

JADEN'S DREAM

Dark clouds floated in the night sky that surrounded Academy Island. A crescent moon glowed dimly from behind the clouds. Beneath the sky, a small wooden boat floated in the gray waters.

A flock of dark creatures flapped their wings above the boat. From a distance, they looked like birds. But closer, it was clear they were bats.

At first, it seemed as if the boat had no passenger, just a simple wood coffin. Then the coffin's lid slowly slid open. The bats began to dance in excitement.

The coffin's inhabitant sat up. Her pale skin was as white as the moon. She had long, flowing green hair and fierce red eyes. Her ears were strangely pointed, and her outfit was even stranger.

A thick metal band circled her neck, and a bat-shaped medallion decorated her red dress. She held a red rose in her hands.

Then she smiled, revealing a set of sharp, pearly fangs. . . .

"*Aaaaaaah!*" Jaden Yuki woke with a start.

His good friend Syrus hovered over the bed where Jaden slept. Worry showed in his blue eyes.

"Jaden, are you okay?" he asked.

"Weird dream," Jaden said. "I saw a . . . girl . . ."

Fontaine, the teacher in charge of the medical center, smiled at Jaden. "You must be feeling better if you're dreaming about girls," she teased.

Jaden closed his eyes. He wasn't sure if he was feeling better. Just a few days ago, he had battled Nightshroud in a Shadow Duel. Every attack had felt *real*—real pain, real suffering. Jaden had drifted in and out of sleep since the duel, too weak to get out of bed.

But he knew someone who was in even worse shape.

Jaden had won the difficult and grueling duel. Nightshroud had collapsed at the end, too, his soul trapped in a card. Then Nightshroud's mask had fallen off, and Alexis, Jaden's friend, had seen his face.

It was her brother. Her very own brother, Atticus, had become a Shadow Rider, one of the duelists sent to take the seven keys from Duel Academy. Whoever held the keys could unlock the legendary Sacred Beasts — monsters with the ability to destroy the world.

Jaden knew Nightshroud — or Atticus, the boy he used to be — was in a nearby bed in the medical center.

Jaden opened his eyes again. "How is Nightshr — I mean, Alexis's brother?" he asked Fontaine.

"I'm afraid he hasn't woken up yet," she replied. "But he's in stable condition."

Jaden nodded and closed his eyes again. He knew how worried Alexis must be. But she had to be strong. They all had to be. Jaden knew what his dream meant.

Another Shadow Rider was coming for them.

On the shores of Academy Island, the boat in Jaden's dreams landed in the sand. The woman stepped out. She looked up at the bats and raised her arms.

"Go, my minions!" she cried. "Find me my prey, so that we may succeed where Nightshroud has failed!"

The bats swirled in one motion, circling the woman.

Then they were gone.

• CHAPTER TWO •

SPIES IN THE NIGHT

Rumors that a mysterious stranger had landed on Academy Island quickly spread through campus.

Some Ra Yellow students talked about it in class.

"Did you hear about the vampire?" one boy asked. "Dude, I saw her with my own two eyes . . . or at least my roommate did."

Some Obelisk Blue students talked as they walked across campus.

"I am so not kidding!" said one girl. "It's a girl vampire!"

"Well, she'd better stay away from my boyfriend!" another girl snapped.

The rumors flew all the way to the office of Chancellor Sheppard, the director of Duel Academy. Sheppard had taken the seven keys guarding the legendary Sacred Beasts and given one each to the school's seven best duelists: Jaden, Alexis, Zane,

Chazz, and Bastion, who were all students, and Dr. Crowler and Professor Banner, both teachers.

Sheppard called the Key Keepers to his office. Jaden and Alexis had to stay in the medical center, but the others arrived and listened to Sheppard's story.

"A vampire?" Chazz asked. His voice clearly showed he didn't believe it.

"I'm afraid the rumors may not be rumors after all," Sheppard said solemnly.

Professor Banner's eyes widened behind his wire glasses. "Oh, my!"

But Dr. Crowler just scowled. "Oh, please! It's a practical joke."

"Joke?" Bastion asked solemnly. "It wasn't a joke that put Jaden in the hospital."

Zane raised an eyebrow. "Do you think she's a Shadow Rider?"

Sheppard nodded. "Perhaps," he replied. "So listen. Be on the lookout for anything strange."

The Key Keepers contemplated Sheppard's warning as they returned to their dorms. Chazz looked through his deck of Duel Masters cards. He smirked as he looked at his powerful lineup of Duel Monsters.

"Let's see this vampire girl try and get the drop on Chazz!" he bragged.

On the wall behind him, a bat stared at Chazz with glowing eyes.

Bastion studied the cards in his deck. Would he be ready to face a Shadow Rider?

A bat hung upside down on a nearby window ledge as well, also studying Bastion.

Zane looked at his cards and sighed, thinking of Jaden in the medical center.

He didn't notice the bat that peered at him through the window.

Dr. Crowler wasn't concerned at all. He sat at his desk, shaking his head in disbelief.

"A vampire?" he chuckled to himself. "What's next, the boogeyman? Who would believe something so ridiculous!"

A bat listened to Crowler's rant, then flew away.

Professor Banner wasn't taking any chances. He had filled his room with bulbs of garlic and burning candles.

"I know you're out there!" Banner called out. "I have a huge horror movie collection. I know all your weak spots!"

The bat hanging from Banner's ceiling made a quick exit.

Back at the medical center, Alexis and Syrus were worried about the vampire . . . in addition to everything else.

"How's Jaden?" Alexis asked Syrus.

"He hasn't said anything since last night," Syrus said. He looked down at Jaden, who slept peacefully in the hospital cot.

"How's your brother, Alexis?" Syrus asked her. His own brother, Zane, was one of the Key Keepers. He knew he'd feel terrible if something bad happened to Zane during a duel. Alexis must be pretty worried.

The girl's gray eyes clouded. "Pretty much the same," she answered. "But he'll get better. I know it. He's a fighter. You know?"

Syrus nodded. "I know."

"I hope the rest are, as well," Alexis said. She looked out the window, into the dark night. "It sounds like the next Shadow Rider is here!"

In an isolated area of Academy Island, the vampire had

found refuge in an abandoned castle in the center of a large black lake. She bathed in a tub filled with water and rose petals. A bat flew through an open window. The vampire lifted up her arm, and the bat landed gently on her finger.

"My precious," she said fondly. "What did you bring me?"

The bat's eyes flashed red, and images of all of the Key Keepers entered the vampire's mind. She contemplated them all, smiling.

"Ah, so this is our opposition," she said. "Who shall it be?"

One of the duelists stood out to her — Zane, with his blue eyes, handsome face, and aura of strong confidence. A truly worthy opponent.

"You," the vampire decided. "You will be my first!"

• CHAPTER THREE •

LET'S DUEL!

Chancellor Sheppard called the Key Keepers back to his office.

"Good news, Chancellor," Chazz began. "I searched the whole campus and there's no —"

"Vampire!"

Jaden's roommate Chumley burst into the office. The heavy boy huffed and panted. "I saw her!" he cried. "She's at the lake!"

Chumley led the Key Keepers to the lake. A gray mist covered the ground, making it nearly impossible to see in the dark night. They gazed out over the water.

Something bright red came toward them over the water. Soon they realized it was a red carpet, unrolling over the lake as if to welcome them.

"I think she's expecting us," Bastion remarked.

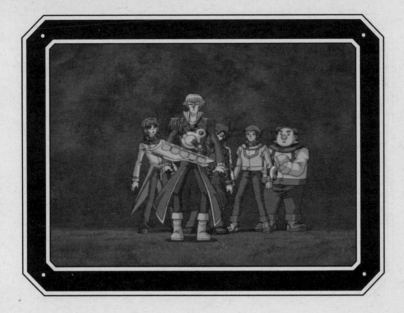

"Crimson red," Zane said. "How fitting."

"What now?" Bastion asked.

"Now we face her," Zane said, his voice filled with determination.

Both Dr. Crowler and Professor Banner were terrified. They slowly began to back up.

The two teachers accidentally backed up into each other. The encounter startled Dr. Crowler, who jumped in front of the Key Keepers. To the rest, it looked as if he had volunteered.

"Oh, wow, Dr. Crowler," Chumley said. "You are so brave."

"We'll be right behind you," Bastion assured him.

"Yes, by a good ten feet," Professor Banner answered.

Chumley raced back to the medical center.

"Syrus!" he cried. "Dr. Crowler's gonna duel against the vampire lady!"

Syrus gasped. "Great, he'll beat her easy, right?"

Alexis shook her head. "Wrong, Sy," she said. "Crowler may talk a big game, but he plays a terrible one."

Jaden woke with a start. Had he heard right? Crowler, battling a Shadow Rider?

Jaden had a long history with Dr. Crowler. Frustrated that he couldn't beat Jaden, the prissy professor had tried to find other duelists to defeat him. Jaden usually came out on top.

Even so, he knew Crowler was a good duelist. But could he stand up to a Shadow Rider? Jaden wasn't so sure.

That meant one of the keys was in danger of falling into the wrong hands. . . .

Back at the lake, the other Key Keepers waited for Crowler to walk down the red carpet.

"So, Crowler, what's the holdup?" Chazz asked.

"If you're in such a hurry, why don't you go first?" Dr. Crowler snapped.

Then a strong wind blew across the lake. The vampire woman appeared out of the mist, riding in her small boat. Bats flew over her head. She stepped out of the boat and began to gracefully glide down the carpet.

"Gentlemen, why don't I just come to you?" she said.

Crowler sneered. Was this a Shadow Rider, or some woman in a cheap costume?

The vampire sized up Crowler. From her point of view, Crowler looked like he was in a costume, with his frilly blue uniform and blond ponytail. "And who might you be?" she asked him.

"I'm your challenger," Crowler replied.

The vampire frowned. *I don't think so,* she thought. *I crave*

another. . . . Her gaze turned to Zane, who looked back at her with steely eyes.

"You are not worthy!" she said out loud.

That made Crowler angry. "I beg your pardon!" he snapped. "I have a Ph.D. in dueling! That takes nine years in duel school, you know!"

"Fine," the vampire replied. "If you're that anxious to lose your key, then you may duel me, Camula, Vampire Mistress of the Shadow Riders."

"Rubber bats and plastic teeth," Crowler shot back. "Your tricks don't scare me."

"Well, then, perhaps this will," Camula challenged. "If you lose, I get your soul. Well, actually, this little doll does."

She held up a small cloth doll with no face.

"You want to take his soul *and* the key?" Bastion asked.

"Forget it!" Chazz cried.

But Crowler wasn't worried. "Is that all?" he asked. "Don't want anything for your mummy? Or perhaps something for your pet werewolf to chew on?"

Camula's lovely face stretched to reveal her sharp fangs. "Be careful what you wish for," she hissed. "It may just come true."

She stared at Crowler. "Now then, Key Keeper," she said. "Let's duel!"

CHAPTER FOUR

THE SWARMING SCOURGE!

Dr. Crowler and Camula activated their Duel Disks. Each duelist began with 4000 life points.

"So, Key Keeper, you don't believe in werewolves?" Camula asked, grinning. She placed a face-up card on her disk. "Perhaps this will convince you. Rise, Zombie Werewolf!"

A piercing howl penetrated the night air as a werewolf appeared on the field in front of Camula. It had gray fur and bloodred eyes. Broken chains hung from its arms. The Duel Monster had 1200 attack points.

"I will end my turn with a facedown card," Camula finished with a mysterious smile.

"Please," Crowler scoffed. "What do you take me for? Some sort of pathetic amateur? That facedown is obviously a trap and that mangy fleabag is clearly the bait! But even so, I'll bite."

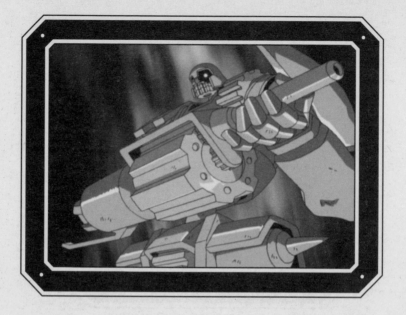

Crowler dramatically put a card on his Duel Disk. The ground began to rumble under the duelists' feet.

"Because you've bitten off more than you can chew!" Crowler cried. "First, I play the spell card Ancient Gear Castle! It gives all my Ancient Gear creatures 300 extra attack points."

The Key Keepers gasped as a huge stone castle rose up behind Crowler. Cannons and other fierce-looking weapons jutted out from the castle's towers.

"And second, I'll play the Ancient Gear Soldier — in attack mode!" Crowler announced. A giant robot made of gray metal appeared next to him. Its eyes glowed with blue light. Thanks to Ancient Gear Castle, its attack points automatically rose from 1300 to 1600.

"And now, Camula," Crowler continued. "It's time we gave

that filthy slobbering mongrel of yours his shots. Attack, Rapid Fire Flurry!"

Ancient Gear Castle aimed a weapon at Zombie Werewolf and pummeled the monster with projectiles. It vanished from the field with a loud cry, and Camula's life points took the extra damage, dropping down to 3600.

Crowler grinned, pleased with himself. "That was fun!" he called to Camula. "I should get out of the classroom more often."

But Camula was smiling, too. "On the contrary, you should study up!" she told him. "Then you'd know that my werewolf is coming back!"

She took a card from her deck, and another Zombie Werewolf appeared, howling.

"But how?" Crowler asked in disbelief.

"Ah, the living," the vampire said. "I forget the ignorance of a beating heart. When Zombie Werewolf is destroyed, I get to summon another from my deck — with 500 more attack points!"

Crowler's pasty face became even paler as he saw the werewolf's attack points leap to 700. On the sidelines, the other Key Keepers looked worried.

"You mean *he* teaches *us*?" Chazz asked.

Crowler turned to the other duelists. "Don't worry, everything is under control!"

He turned back to Camula. "I place one card facedown. I guess it's your turn."

"Why, thank you," the vampire replied. "And I summon Vampire Bat in attack mode!"

Camula waved her hand, and a small army of bats appeared and flapped their wings overhead. Then the bats joined together to form one large Vampire Bat with huge, leathery wings and red eyes. And 800 attack points flashed below it.

"Now, with my winged friend out on the field, every zombie monster I have out gains 200 attack points," Camula announced.

Crowler watched as the Vampire Bat's attack points rose to 1000, and the Zombie Werewolf's points climbed to 1900.

"Don't you three look cute," he taunted. "You know, if you had bags, you could go trick-or-treating!"

"The only treat will be your demise," Camula promised. "Zombie Werewolf, sic that Gear Soldier. Midnight Pounce!"

Zombie Werewolf growled and hurled himself across the field with his muscular legs. There was a huge explosion as he made contact with the Ancient Gear Soldier. When the dust cleared, the soldier was gone, and Crowler's life points dropped down to 3700.

"Well, well," Crowler said, keeping his cool. "It would appear that your mutt still has some bite in him after all. No matter. *I* still have more life points."

"Perhaps, but not for much longer," Camula said. "Vampire Bat, attack with Swarming Scourge!"

The bat squealed loudly in reply. It divided up into smaller bats once again, and they flew across the field and surrounded Crowler, biting and scratching him. The professor raised his arms to protect his face.

I can actually feel their little teeth, Crowler realized with growing horror. *This isn't some dueling hologram. This is real. And that can only mean one thing . . . this is really a Shadow Game duel!*

◆ CHAPTER FIVE ◆

INFERNALVANIA!

Back at the medical center, Syrus watched the duel on the screen of his communication device while Alexis looked on. Jaden slept nearby.

"Crowler's taking a beating," he announced.

"No! He can't!" Alexis cried. "If Crowler doesn't win, he'll lose his key *and* his soul."

The words penetrated Jaden's cloudy mind. He had dueled so hard and risked so much to protect his key from Nightshroud. The keys couldn't fall into the wrong hands. The fate of the world depended on it.

Jaden slowly opened his eyes. He had to do something . . . before it was too late.

On the shores of the lake, Crowler struggled to get to his feet. Camula laughed at his pain.

"For rubber bats, they pack quite a wallop, don't they?" she said. "Listen, dear, you don't have to endure this. Step down, and I'll duel the one in white." She looked directly at Zane.

"You hear that, Zane? It sounds like you're her type," Chazz said.

"Yes, or her *blood* type," Banner added.

"So how about it?" Camula asked. "Give me your student, and I'll let you go free."

"As tempting as your offer is, I don't think so!" Crowler cried angrily. He shakily stood up and glared at Camula. "I won't let you lay a finger on my students! I am the leading professor at the most famous duel academy in the world. If you want to get to my pupils, you have to get through yours truly!"

"But you can barely stand, Crowler!" Chazz pointed out.

Crowler grimaced in pain. "Don't worry about me," he said. "I still have a deck in my hand, and a few tricks up my sleeve."

He turned over his facedown card. "I play Damage Condenser!" he cried. The card face showed a machine comprised of glass tubes and pipes. "It summons a monster from my graveyard whose attack points are equal or less than the damage you've just inflicted on me. In other words, the more pain you deal, the more hurt you'll feel!"

"And you'll be feeling it soon," Crowler continued, his voice filled with newfound strength. "Rise, Ancient Gear Soldier!"

Ancient Gear Soldier appeared on the field once again.

"But he won't be around for long," Crowler said. "I'll now

sacrifice Ancient Gear Soldier so I can summon my own four-legged friend: Ancient Gear Beast!"

A giant robot dog appeared on the field, its metal body shining purple and silver in the moonlight. Next to the monster, 2300 attack points flashed.

"Go, Ancient Gear Beast!" Crowler cried. "Show that Zombie Werewolf who's top dog!"

"Don't do it!" Chazz called from the sidelines. "If you win, she'll bring the werewolf back all over again!"

"Appreciate the advice, but you're forgetting his special ability," Crowler said. "Ancient Gear Beast cancels the effect of any destroyed monster."

Bastion nodded, impressed. "Clever calculation."

"Yes! Good thinking," Professor Banner agreed.

Dr. Crowler turned back to his Duel Monster. "Now, attack Zombie Werewolf!"

The mechanical beast sprang into action. It jumped across the field and bit Zombie Werewolf with its sharp metal teeth.

The werewolf's pained howl echoed across the field as it vanished from sight. For the first time, Camula frowned.

"If you'd like some help with your dueling strategy, feel free to stop by my class," Crowler taunted.

Camula's frown quickly turned into an evil giggle. "Nice move," she said. "Pity you won't have many more. I cast the field spell Infernalvania!"

As Camula threw down the card, a stone castle rose up behind her. It looked dark and spooky.

Crowler gasped. "But you'll destroy everything with that!"

"Exactly," the vampire said. "By discarding a zombie

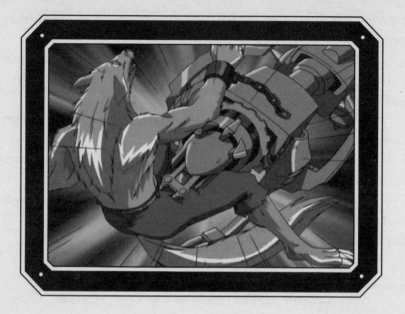

monster from my hand, I can send every creature that is on the field straight to the graveyard."

"That's true," Chazz called out. "But by using Infernalvania, you're not going to be able to normal summon your monsters anymore."

"So what? Who says I need any more monsters?" Camula replied. She looked at Crowler, challenging him. "Isn't that right?"

"Don't play games with me," Crowler said. "I know all about that bat of yours."

"But do your students?" Camula asked. "Do they know Vampire Bat can be made indestructible by simply discarding another one from my deck? Or did you skip that chapter?"

The Key Keepers exchanged glances. An indestructible monster . . . that was something to worry about.

"First, I'll discard one of my zombie monsters to activate Infernalvania," Camula said, taking a card from her deck. Vampire Lord appeared briefly, and then vanished into the graveyard. "And I'll discard another Vampire Bat to keep this one on my field."

The giant bat hovered above the vampire's head. Crowler cringed, remembering the last attack. Camula grinned to see his fear.

"Now attack the good professor!" she ordered.

Vampire Bat turned into an army of bats once again, and they descended on Dr. Crowler, squealing and biting.

"No, not again!" Crowler wailed, covering his face.

Zane stepped forward. "He needs our help."

"No!" Crowler insisted. "Stay back! This is my duel, and my duel alone. You must protect your keys. . . ."

Crowler's life points dropped to 1700. He fell face forward

onto the ground. The bats flew away, leaving his motionless body on the field.

"We can't just stand here and do nothing!" Zane said angrily.

"Yes, I completely agree with you, darling," Camula said. "Please step in. Save your teacher, because obviously he can't save himself."

"Wrong!"

All eyes turned to the sound of the voice. It was Jaden! Chumley carried him on his back. Syrus ran behind them.

"Dr. Crowler can win this duel," Jaden insisted. "I know because I've dueled him. Believe me, he can throw down!"

Crowler's body stirred slightly on the field.

"So get up, Dr. Crowler!" Jaden yelled. "And get your game on!"

• CHAPTER SIX •

VAMPIRE GENESIS

Jaden's words revived Crowler. The professor struggled to his feet.

"I am not giving up!" he growled.

"Oh, are you still here?" Camula asked.

"You had better believe it," Crowler replied. "And here to stay, too, missy! You see, though it makes me slightly ill to admit, Jaden is absolutely right! I can beat you! I can throw down! And I can get my game on!"

Dr. Crowler paused. Had he actually uttered Jaden's catch-phrase? "*Blehk*, I suddenly feel the need to rinse out my mouth."

"It's not *that* bad, teach!" Jaden called out.

Crowler turned to Camula. "Now, let's duel!" he cried. "I summon Ancient Gear Golem in attack mode!"

Another mechanical monster appeared in the field, but

this one was larger than any of Crowler's others. It stood as tall as the towers of the Ancient Gear Castle, and wore a metal suit of armor. One red eye shone from underneath its helmet. An impressive 3000 attack points flashed next to it.

"Crowler's best monster!" Chazz said, impressed.

"But where's the sacrifice?" Syrus asked.

"It's on the field," Zane explained. "The Ancient Gear Castle. A very skillful move. See, when summoning a monster with *ancient* in the name, you can sacrifice Ancient Gear Castle, and it counts as the same number of sacrifices as however many monsters you've summoned so far."

As Zane spoke, the castle vanished from the field.

"Now, Gear Golem, attack Vampire Bat with Mechanized Melee!" Crowler cried.

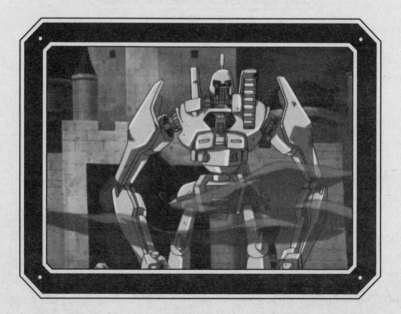

Ancient Gear Golem pulled back one massive fist, then pounded the bat with a mighty blow. The bat disappeared, and Camula's life points dropped down to 1200.

"Did you forget that Vampire Bat can't be destroyed?" she asked him.

"I'm afraid you're mistaken," Crowler replied calmly.

"What's he gonna do?" Chazz wondered.

"Oh, just destroy every trap and spell card on the entire field!" the professor announced. "Suffer the wrath of Heavy Storm!"

Crowler triumphantly held up the Heavy Storm card, and a strong wind blew across the field. It knocked down Infernalvania, and sent Camula's trap and spell cards flying.

The Key Keepers watched, impressed. Had Crowler done it? Was this the end of Camula?

But the vampire just grinned. "You must be quite a bore for your students. So predictable!"

"Please! You don't know what you're talking about," Crowler protested.

"Oh, don't I?" Camula said. Her face contorted into the hideous face of a vampire monster. "I activate the trap Zombie Bed!"

"You can't!" Crowler cried. "I just destroyed all the trap and spell cards!"

"Which is exactly what I wanted you to do," Camula said.

Zane nodded from the sidelines. "Of course, it's obvious. In order to be activated, Zombie Bed has to be destroyed!"

"Very good, my darling," Camula purred. "And now that it has been activated, its effect lets me summon back Zombie Werewolf in attack mode!"

The howling werewolf appeared, with 1400 attack points.

"And because *your* card got rid of all trap and spell cards, you're completely defenseless," Camula pointed out.

"She knows Crowler's every move even before *he* does," Chazz remarked.

The vampire laughed. "It's easy when you have a hundred flying bats spying on everyone," she said. One of her winged spies landed on her shoulder. Then her smile faded. "It's over, Crowler! I activate Book of Life. It resurrects my Vampire Lord."

Camula threw down a card with Egyptian markings. Vampire Lord, the card she had sacrificed earlier, appeared on the field.

"However, you can't give life without taking it away," she continued. "So I'll be taking your Ancient Gear Beast from your grave so you can't use him again!"

Crowler sighed nervously. He could see where this was leading . . . and it didn't look good.

Camula made her next move. "Now I'm removing Vampire Lord from play, so that I can summon Vampire Genesis!"

There was a gasp from the onlookers as the half-bat, half-human monster appeared. Its purple body was heavily muscled, and red eyes shone in its monstrous face. The creature boasted 3000 attack points — the same as Crowler's Ancient Gear Golem. The card was the final evolution of all vampire cards, an unbeatable combination of supernatural being and beast.

"And since Vampire Bat is still on the field, his attack points increase by 200," Camula finished.

Dr. Crowler winced. That meant Vampire Genesis now

had 3200 attack points, 200 more than his Golem. He knew what was about to come. The vampire had massive amounts of attack power on the field, and he had no defenses, no traps, no spells. He slowly turned to face the Key Keepers.

"My students, no matter what happens to me, always remember this," he said. "I may have been hard on you at times, but it's simply because I believe in you. Therefore, if I fall here, there's still hope. Because I know you all will rise."

"Don't talk like that!" Zane cried.

"Have you finished your final lesson yet, Crowler?" Camula called out.

Crowler turned around. "Excuse me, but that's *Doctor* to you!"

"If you wish," she replied. "I'll put it on your tombstone as soon as I'm finished. Vampire Genesis, destroy his Golem!"

Ancient Gear Golem shattered into pieces. Crowler cried out as his life points dropped to 1500.

"No!" Zane cried.

"That all?" Crowler asked bravely. "I thought you Shadow Riders were supposed to be tough."

"You want more?" Camula laughed. "Very well!"

She pointed to Zombie Werewolf. The creature jumped up and slashed Crowler. The professor screamed in agony. His life points quickly fell to 100.

And Camula still was not finished.

"Here, try this as well!" she cried. "Vampire Bat, attack!"

The flock of bats attacked Crowler for the third time, swarming around his face. The professor moaned. The Key Keepers watched in horror as his life points dropped to zero.

Crowler looked at Jaden. "Avenge me, my boy," he said weakly.

Then he collapsed.

Camula grinned triumphantly. "His key is mine."

CHAPTER SEVEN

ONE DOWN

Chazz stepped forward, his fists clenched. "No way!"

"We can't stop her," Jaden said. "She won the duel."

Camula stepped over Crowler's still body. She reached down and took the key from around his neck.

"One down, and six to go," she said. She stared at the key, and it quickly vanished. "And now, darling children, to take my second prize."

The vampire held the small cloth doll over Crowler's body. A purple mist swirled from the fallen professor and entered the doll. Now the doll's blank face bore the unnatural grin of Dr. Crowler, and his uniform covered the doll's body.

"She put Crowler's soul in a doll," Syrus said, horrified.

"Dolls are pretty," Camula said. "This is decidedly not. It's garbage now." She tossed the doll on the ground.

"That's it!" Jaden cried angrily. He wanted to duel — now!

But Zane put an arm in front of Jaden, blocking his way.

"Now I bid farewell!" Camula cried. She floated up into the air, surrounded by her bats.

Then they all vanished.

"We'll find you!" Bastion cried out.

"And duel!" Chazz added.

The vampire's laugh came from nowhere, echoing in their ears.

"Children, that is precisely what I'm hoping for!"

◄ CHAPTER EIGHT ►

ANOTHER BITE

Late the next day, the Key Keepers gathered around Jaden's hospital bed. The trip to witness Dr. Crowler's battle had weakened him. He lay on his back, exhausted — and angry.

"I'll play a trap, and then a spell, and then I'll attack!" he cried, plotting out his battle with Camula. He tried to sit up, then grimaced in pain. "Well, just as soon as I get better, I will."

"Jay, you really ought to rest," Syrus said, worried.

"Sy's right," Professor Banner agreed. He stroked his large ginger cat, Pharaoh. "If we're not at our best, it's *our* souls that will be sealed in those dolls, and our bodies will be catatonic!"

Pharaoh jumped out of Banner's arms with alarm and dashed under Jaden's bed. Banner bent down to coax him out.

"No, Pharaoh, just because the word has *cat* in it doesn't

mean it applies to you," he assured his pet. "Though I'm not sure nine lives makes a difference with vampires."

Bastion stood next to Banner, his arms folded. With his neatly combed hair and crisp Ra Yellow uniform, the student looked all business, as usual.

"The worst part is, since Camula was able to take Crowler's key, she needs just six more to unleash those Beast cards," he said thoughtfully.

Alexis sat by the side of her brother's bed. "And then it won't be our souls at stake, but everyone's in the world!" she pointed out.

"That's it!" Jaden cried. "I'm dueling her — tonight!"

Chazz sat on a chair close to Jaden, holding in his hand the doll that held Crowler's soul. His spiky black hair and black uniform gave him a gloomy appearance, and his gray eyes were clouded with concern. But they burned with fire at Jaden's threat.

"You duel? Think again!" Chazz said. He pulled Jaden's sheet over the boy's face. "You can't even win a fight with a sheet. This duel is for the Chazz."

Jaden grappled with the material for a moment, and then stuck his face out. "There! I won!"

"You did not," Chazz said, covering Jaden's face again. "It's two out of three."

Jaden struggled to get the sheet off of him. Chazz had made his point.

"Look, Jaden's not up to snuff," he said. "One of us is going to have to face Camula."

Alexis stood up. "What we need is to work together," she said firmly. "Protecting the keys and getting Crowler's soul back is all that matters."

Jaden freed himself from the sheet. "All right," he admitted. "I'll sit out . . . till I get better."

The other Key Keepers nodded in agreement — except one. Syrus noticed his brother, Zane, leave quietly through the door. He ran after him.

"Didn't we just decide to work together?" Syrus asked. "Where are you going?"

Zane looked over his shoulder and grinned at his little brother.

"If all that matters is protecting those keys and rescuing Crowler, you know where I'm going."

Syrus watched his brother disappear down the hallway. Zane had never lost a duel. He'd even beaten Jaden, one of the best in Duel Academy. But could he take down Camula?

The Key Keepers went back to their dorms. Chazz sat on the bed in his room, arranging the cards in his deck. As he worked, a small, yellow spirit flew out of the deck and circled his face. The little creature had a chubby body and eyes on the end of two long stalks. Chazz sighed.

His road to becoming a great duelist had been filled with ups and downs. At one low point, the spirit of a card, Ojama Yellow, had appeared to help him. Even though the card could sometimes be helpful, Chazz mostly felt the spirit was annoying.

"Hey, long time, boss! How's things! What are you doing? Arranging your deck? Can I help?" Ojama Yellow asked.

Chazz grunted and flicked the spirit away. Ojama Yellow bounced on the belly of the cloth doll that held Dr. Crowler's soul.

"Hey, fragile here!"

Ojama Yellow looked at the doll. The voice was definitely Crowler's, although the doll's lips weren't moving. Curious, he tickled the doll's arm.

"What are you doing? Stop it!" the doll protested.

Ojama Yellow quickly flew to Chazz. "Boss! This doll's alive!"

Chazz picked up the doll.

"Would you mind easing up on the grip a tad? You're wrinkling my coat!" the doll said, although Chazz could see it wasn't really talking. Crowler's voice was somehow coming out of it.

"That's Dr. Crowler, all right," Chazz agreed.

Another sound got Ojama Yellow's attention. He floated to the window — and saw the night sky filled with countless flapping bats. Chazz ran outside.

"It's starting again!"

The other Key Keepers saw it, too. Chumley hoisted Jaden onto his back.

"Run!" Jaden yelled.

"Aw, *running*?" Chumley asked.

"Whatever you do, let's get a move on," Alexis said. "I have a feeling that vampire is about to bite again!"

◆ CHAPTER NINE ◆

POWER BOND!

Chumley and Syrus headed back to the lake with the Key Keepers. Only Zane wasn't with them. They could see him up ahead, walking determinedly across the red carpet into the mist.

As they came closer, they could see where the carpet led: to a huge stone castle, its many turrets jutting up into the clouds. The castle sat on a rocky island in the lake.

"Explain to me again why we're going *to* this place, instead of running away from it . . . or walking away?" Chumley asked.

The others ignored Chumley's complaints. They caught up to Zane and followed him through the castle's massive front door. A steep stone staircase rose in front of them. They climbed up and entered a hallway lined with flaming torches.

Then the hallway opened up into a large, old ballroom. There was no furniture, no carpet — just a rickety chandelier hanging from the ceiling. Across the ballroom, a balcony extended from the wall. Camula stepped out of the darkness and walked to the balcony's edge.

"Ah, right on time," the vampire said. "Looking for me?"

"You bet we are!" Jaden cried. "We want Crowler back!"

"Got that right!" Chazz said. "So hand him over!"

"Or else!" Bastion warned.

Camula dismissively waved her hand. "I have no interest in little schoolboys," she said. She fixed her gaze on Zane. "Are you ready, darling?"

Zane stared back at her, his face a mask that showed no fear.

"Let's duel," he said firmly.

Zane walked to the other side of the ballroom and climbed up to a balcony facing Camula.

"Good luck, bro," Syrus whispered.

"Let us review," Camula began. "If you win, you get Crowler's soul back and I'll be on my way. But if *I* win, I get *your* soul and your spirit key, and I get to continue my quest to unleash the three Sacred Beasts!"

Zane nodded. The two duelists activated their Duel Disks. Each one started with 4000 life points.

"I like to lead," Camula called out. "I summon Vampire Lady in defense mode!"

She placed the card on her Duel Disk, and an image of the card floated in front of her. Vampire Lady looked like an old-fashioned version of Camula, with a fancy purple dress. Her long, green hair was piled on top of her head. Then 1550 defense points popped up next to her.

"And I'll lay one card facedown," Camula continued. "That's all."

Zane raised an eyebrow. "Really? Shame. Because it won't be enough to protect you from what *I* have planned." He held up a card.

Camula recognized it. "Playing Power Bond?" she asked, surprised.

"It allows me to fuse machine-type monsters," Zane replied. "And I have the perfect three in mind — my Cyber Dragons!"

Three robot dragons appeared behind Zane. Their long, snakelike necks were covered with silver metal scales. They roared loudly.

"Now unite, and form the almighty Cyber End Dragon!" Zane cried.

A flash of white light flooded the ballroom, and the three

dragons were replaced by a massive three-headed dragon. The neck of each dragon was adorned in gleaming metal scales of different colors: gold, blue, and green. Two large metal wings grew from its back. Next to the beast flashed 4000 attack points.

The onlookers gasped.

"Zane's summoned his most powerful monster on his very first turn!" Alexis cried.

Syrus wondered what his brother was thinking. *Wow, that's not like Zane*, he thought. *He usually feels out an opponent before throwing Power Bond. It's almost like he's just using it instead of playing it. I hope he knows what he's doing. . . .*

Camula seemed to think the move was amusing. "My, I like your aggressiveness," she said. "But Power Bond has its risks. Are you certain you can handle all the consequences?"

Chumley nodded on the floor below. "She's right," he realized. "At the turn's end, Zane will take damage equal to Cyber's original attack points. And that adds up to 4000 big ones! But that may be a risk he's willing to take because now Power Bond doubles Cyber End Dragon's attack points."

As Chumley said it, Cyber End Dragon's attack points leaped to 8000.

"I don't think I'll have to worry about consequences after this turn," Zane said matter-of-factly. "Attack Vampire Lady, Super Strident Blaze!"

Each head of the dragon opened its mouth. Golden light began to form, ready for the attack. But Camula held up a card with a moon face on it.

"Forgetting my facedown?" she asked. "I play the trap Red Ghost Moon! By discarding one zombie in my hand to the graveyard, *your* monster's attack points are added directly to my life points."

The moon card appeared on the field in front of Vampire Lady. Waves of golden light hurled across the room toward the cards, but instead of harming Vampire Lady, the light glittered brightly around Camula.

"That's 8000 points from your dragon, plus the 4000 I had, giving me a total of 12,000 points!" Camula crowed triumphantly.

But Zane's turn was not over yet.

"Wrong," he said calmly. "I activate the spell card De-Fusion, disassembling Cyber End Dragon and leaving you with absolutely nothing. Red Ghost Moon's target is gone, so its effect is canceled!"

"My points!" Camula cried, as her life points dropped back down to 4000.

Syrus watched from the floor below, impressed. A while ago, Zane had said that Syrus wasn't a good enough duelist to be at Duel Academy. That had hurt. But there was no question that Zane was one of the best duelists around. His last move proved it.

"Now that Power Bond is gone . . ." Syrus began.

"He won't have to pay points for using it!" Chumley finished.

"Now *that's* playing a card!" Jaden added.

The large dragon behind Zane broke down into three separate dragons once again. Zane took one more card from his hand and placed it on his Duel Disk.

"I'll end with one facedown," he said.

Camula just giggled. "Oh, my darling! I can see why you're ranked the top duelist at Duel Academy."

"You haven't seen anything yet," Zane replied.

"I hope not," Camula said. "Zane dear, we've only just begun this duel. And I expect to have a lot more *fun* with you!"

Something in the tone of her voice made Syrus shudder. "I don't think I'm gonna like her kind of fun!" he said nervously.

• CHAPTER TEN •

CYBER LASER DRAGON

Camula began her turn in her usual dramatic fashion.

"Now then, shall we?" she asked. "First, I'll sacrifice Vampire Lady to summon Vampire Lord."

Vampire Lady vanished in a flash, and was replaced by a tall vampire in a purple cape.

"Next I'll sacrifice him to summon Vampire Genesis!"

Vampire Lord disappeared, and Camula's superpowerful half-bat, half-vampire appeared in front of her, roaring with battle lust.

"Ugly!" Chazz remarked.

"Scary!" Syrus added, shivering.

"Darling Zane," Camula purred. "I promised you some fun, didn't I? And now we'll have it. Are you excited?"

Zane didn't respond. He stared back at the vampire with his icy blue eyes.

"Oh, you're such a bore," Camula sighed. "Maybe this will rouse you — Vampire Genesis, attack!"

Vampire Genesis charged across the room.

"As·*fun* as this is, I'm afraid I'm going to have to interrupt it with my facedown card," Zane said. "The trap Attack Reflector Unit!"

"A trap?" Camula asked.

"One that's evolutionary," Zane replied. "You see, Attack Reflector Unit evolves my Cyber Dragon into the Cyber Barrier Dragon!"

As Zane spoke, one of Zane's dragons transformed into a dragon with a smaller, snakelike head. A metal hood framed the new dragon's face, and the scales on its metal body gleamed like

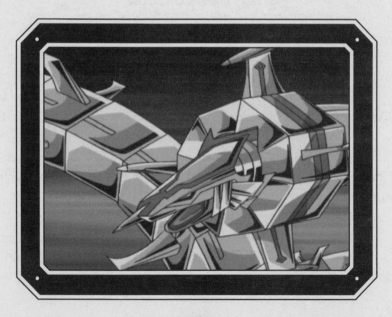

hundreds of blinding mirrors. The monster had 800 attack points.

"When the Cyber Barrier Dragon is in attack mode, once per turn, it allows me to negate the attack of your monster," Zane announced. "So your Vampire Genesis's attack can go right back to where it started!"

Cyber Barrier Dragon's body glowed brightly as Vampire Genesis approached it. Then a stream of light reflected from its body, slamming into Vampire Genesis. The great beast stood in front of Camula once more.

"How dare you!" Camula angrily spat out the words.

Down on the floor, Jaden grinned. "Your bro's got game!" he said. "No wonder he beat me. Though it *was* close."

"It's my turn!" Zane said. "And I play Pot of Greed. This lets me draw two cards from my deck."

Zane took the two cards.

"Next I activate the spell card Photon Generator Unit," he said. "Now by sacrificing my dragons, I can summon the Cyber Laser Dragon."

Zane's two dragons flashed off the field and were replaced by a larger dragon with a sleeker body. Its powerful body was coiled, as though ready to pounce into action. Next to it flashed 2400 attack points.

"With Cyber Laser Dragon, once every turn, I can destroy a monster that has equal or more attack or defense points than Laser Dragon's attack points!"

"I bet you talk to all the girls like that," Camula said.

"No, just ones I really don't like!" Zane replied. "Now, Laser Dragon. Let loose with Blue Lightning Lash!"

A spiraling tunnel of blue light shot from Laser Dragon and wrapped around Vampire Genesis. The monster's cries shook

the ballroom as it vanished from the field. Amazingly, Laser Dragon was able to destroy Vampire Genesis, even though Vampire Genesis had more attack points.

"Now go ahead and attack her directly!" Zane ordered his monster.

Another tornado of blue laser light spiraled across the room, whirling around Camula. She wailed as her life points drained to 1600.

"And don't think I forgot my Cyber Barrier Dragon," Zane said, nodding to his other monster on the field. "Attack! Sonic Shriek!"

A painful, high-pitched squeal came from Cyber Barrier Dragon, powered by waves of green and white light. The blast sent Camula flying backward. She slammed into the wall behind her and then landed, her whole body shaking. Now the vampire had only 800 life points left — and Zane still had all of his.

"All right!" Syrus cheered. Camula was almost beaten. That meant Dr. Crowler could get his soul back.

And the Key Keepers would never have to face Camula again.

• CHAPTER ELEVEN •

AN IMPOSSIBLE CHOICE

A surge of hope flooded everyone watching the battle.

"That's exactly the move I would have made!" Chumley bragged.

"Sure, Chum," Jaden teased. "In your dreams!"

"So now you can see why my brother's never lost," Syrus said. "Still, Mom says I got the looks."

Jaden and Chumley just shook their heads.

Up on his balcony, Zane finished his turn with a face-down card.

Camula walked to the front of her balcony. "Darling, you do realize you're forcing me to reveal my ugly side," she said. Her face stretched as it had during the battle with Crowler, making her look like the monster she really was. "And it's only going to get uglier. I play Illusion Gate!"

Camula held up a card, and behind her a stone gate rose up. The gate was carved with clouds and lightning bolts and topped with a stone sculpture of a bat.

"I've never heard of Illusion Gate," Jaden said. "You guys know what it does?"

"I think we're about to find out," Professor Banner remarked.

"Behold!" Camula cried. "First, this spell card destroys all monsters on your field."

Zane flinched slightly as his two dragons disappeared.

"But that's not all," the vampire giggled. "It has twin functions."

To help illustrate her point, a duplicate of Camula appeared next to the vampire. She looked identical, down to the evil grin on her face.

"This card allows me to summon any monster you've used during the entire duel," Camula continued. "So even though you defused Cyber Dragon after only one turn, you did use him during this duel."

"Please," Zane said. "No card is powerful enough to let you make a move like that. There must be some kind of catch."

"Yes, but it's just a tiny one," Camula admitted. "After using Illusion Gate, should I happen to still lose this duel, I must sacrifice a soul to the Sacred Beasts!"

"Well, good!" Chazz called out. "It's what you get for taking Crowler's soul!"

Camula grinned. "Beg your pardon," she said. "I said *a* soul, not *my* soul. You see, in the shadows, it's all the same to the Sacred Beasts."

She looked down at the onlookers, and her pale eyes focused on one of them. "Syrus," she hissed. "Oh, yes. Those beasts would find your soul to be a tasty treat, I'm sure."

"Syrus! Run!" Zane yelled.

But Syrus was paralyzed with fear. Before he could act, Camula's double flew down from the balcony. She grabbed Syrus and carried him to the balcony.

"Sy!" Zane cried.

Syrus felt defeated, frightened, and weak, as though the vampire double were draining his energy. "Sorry, Zane."

"And now I summon the almighty Cyber End Dragon!" Camula shrieked.

Zane's three-headed monster appeared next to Camula. All three heads roared in anticipation of their next move.

"Whatever will you do?" Camula taunted him. "I have your best monster *and* your little brother."

Zane grunted as the seriousness of the situation began to sink in.

"Actually, I suppose they're one and the same now," Camula continued. "After all, if you somehow manage to do in the Cyber End Dragon, you'll also be doing in little Syrus's soul. So, as I said, whatever will you do?"

Anger burned inside Zane like a flame. He faced an impossible choice.

The facedown card on my field is Call of the Haunted, he thought. *If I use it to resurrect Cyber Barrier Dragon, I can stop that Cyber End Dragon and win the duel. Camula will be defeated.*

We'll be that much closer to keeping the world safe from those Sacred Beasts. And in exchange, we lose just one soul. My brother's.

Zane sighed.

The choice is clear.

• CHAPTER TWELVE •

A HERO FALLS

"So, what is it going to be?" Camula asked Zane. "Save the world? Or save your brother's soul — which also means losing yours!"

Syrus looked down at his brother. "Go on, Zane, do it," he said weakly. "You have to. My soul is a small price to pay to stop Camula. After all, if she wins this duel, Zane, she'll get your spirit key. And you know what that means. . . ."

Zane looked at his little brother, transfixed. Could Syrus really be so brave?

"The Shadow Riders will be much closer to freeing those Sacred Beasts," Syrus said. "And besides, if one of us has to go down, it might as well be me. Sure, I may have gotten the looks, but the truth is, you got just about everything else. The skills, the smarts, everything."

Although the brothers were across the ballroom, Zane felt there was no distance between them.

"At least this way I'll be remembered for something other than being your little brother," Syrus added. "I'll be the one who's the hero. After all, we both know I would never have been able to do it by dueling. It's just like you said, bro. I never belonged here."

"I did say that, Syrus, but since then, you've proved me wrong," Zane said gently. "You *do* belong here."

Syrus's blue eyes grew wide with surprise. Did Zane really mean it?

"I love you, Syrus. Never forget it," Zane said. "I'll miss you, little bro. Farewell."

Syrus closed his eyes, ready to lose his soul to Camula.

Zane stared down the vampire from across the room. Now, for certain, he knew what choice he had to make. The only choice he *could* make.

"I stand down," he said. He lowered his Duel Disk.

"Zane! What are you doing?" Syrus cried.

"So be it!" Camula yelled. "Cyber End Dragon, destroy him!"

A pulsating ball of golden light shot from the mouth of each of Cyber End Dragon's three heads. The light balls blazed with heat and energy. They slammed into Zane with incredible force. His body shook violently from the attack.

"Stop! Take *me*!" Syrus screamed.

Zane's key flew off of his neck and clattered onto the ballroom floor. His life points dropped to zero, and he collapsed.

"Zane, no!" Bastion yelled.

They all watched in horror as Zane's eyes went blank. A purple mist circled his body, and then it slowly vanished.

On the balcony, Syrus stared as the purple mist swirled around the small, cloth doll in Camula's hand. The nightmare continued as the doll took on the features of his brother.

"No!" Syrus wailed. He fell to his knees in despair.

Camula smiled at the doll in her hand. "At last, darling, you're all mine," she said. "A tad smaller, and a smidge less talk-ative, but a darling trophy nonetheless."

Then she laughed, a loud, nasty laugh that bounced off the walls of the ballroom. A cold wind whipped up, and Camula flew off with it as her laugh faded away.

Slowly, and in shock, the Key Keepers, Syrus, and Chumley walked out of the castle. When they reached the shore of the

lake, they turned and stared at the castle. How could Zane be gone?

Jaden broke the stunned silence.

"That's it!" he yelled. He jumped off Chumley's back and landed on his knees in the dirt. "No more, Camula! I'm through with you messing with my friends! Got that? What you did to Crowler, to Zane? It stops here! And I'm going to be the one who stops it!"

"Jaden —" Alexis warned. She could see he was so weak that his hands were trembling. Jaden clutched the grass beneath his fingers until his knuckles turned white.

"I may not be up to snuff, but I don't care," Jaden said. His voice turned to a scream. "I'm taking you on, and one way or another, I'm getting our friends' souls back!"

"About time!" the Crowler doll said.

Jaden slowly rose to his feet. He stood tall for the first time since his battle with Nightshroud.

"Camula!" he yelled. "Here I come. So get set to get your game on!"

◆ CHAPTER THIRTEEN ◆

THIRD TIME'S THE CHARM

The next evening, Chancellor Sheppard stared out of his office window, worried. As the head of Duel Academy, he was charged with guarding the three Sacred Beast cards, safely stored in an underground tomb below the island. But two of the spirit gates had been opened. If the other five keys were lost, the beasts would be unleashed. . . .

A sound of static from his computer made him turn around. A face, shrouded in darkness, had appeared on his computer screen. Sheppard knew this was his shadowy nemesis — the evil force that sought to free the beasts.

"You disappoint me," the mysterious figure said. "Your 'excellent' duelists excel only at losing! Why don't you give up and surrender the remaining five keys now?"

"It's not over," Sheppard said firmly. "And if I know my

students, they'll never give up. No matter what the odds. After all, they've come to this island to be champions."

"And they'll end up victims," the villain said, his voice filled with contempt. "My vampire is ready to feed again. . . ."

Back in the medical center, Jaden tossed and turned in his bed once more. His determination to take down Camula hadn't left him, but his body was still weak from his shadow duel with Nightshroud.

Alexis hovered over him. She hardly left the medical center these days, between looking after Jaden and staying by her brother's side, hoping he would wake up.

"Get well," she whispered to Jaden. "With my brother still unconscious and Zane's soul stolen, we'll need all the help we can get to fight the Shadow Games and that vampire Camula."

Alexis heard a sound from her brother's bed. She turned

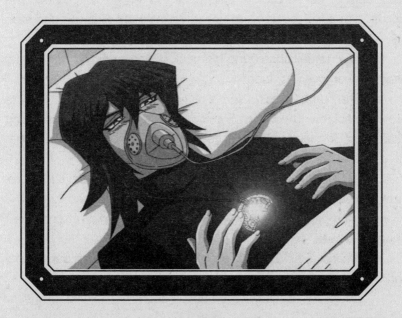

to see that the medallion he wore around his neck was glowing. Alexis had been curious about the medallion, which looked like a gold coin broken in half. Jaden had a similar one around his neck as well. He had obtained it during a shadow duel with the Gravekeeper.

"Atticus?" Alexis asked.

Then, to her amazement, her brother's brown eyes fluttered open.

Alexis quickly took the oxygen mask off his face.

"Atticus! You're awake!" she cried.

"Alexis," Atticus said weakly. "I need to tell you about *her*. The vampire known as Camula. You cannot defeat her like the others."

"But why not?" Alexis asked.

"She has a Shadow Charm that gives her the power to steal souls," her brother replied. He struggled to get out the words. "I'm sure you've seen her use it already. But you can stop her with another charm. . . ."

The medallion around his neck began to glow once more. Alexis looked over at Jaden.

She knew what to do.

Back at the lake, Syrus and Chumley were dragging Professor Banner to the red carpet that led to Camula's castle. He clutched his cat tightly in his arms.

"Come on, Professor Banner, you have to duel that vampire!" Syrus told him. "I mean, you're a Shadow Games expert!"

"And you're the only one wearing garlic aftershave," Chumley added.

"I can't duel!" Banner protested. "Who will take care of my cat? Pharaoh has a very specific diet!"

Chazz and Bastion stood at the shore of the lake, amused.

"Don't worry about it, Banner," Chazz said. The Crowler doll stuck out of his jacket pocket. "This is clearly a job for Chazz Princeton, anyway!"

"If you mean feeding the cat, I think you're right," Bastion remarked.

Before a duelist could be chosen, a speedboat raced toward them. Alexis was steering.

"The cavalry's here!" she called out. "We don't need Banner when we've got . . . Jaden!"

Jaden stood up in the boat. "What's up!"

Syrus shook his head. "For the last time, you can't!"

"Yeah, you're still hurt, slacker!" Chazz pointed out.

Alexis and Jaden exchanged glances.

"Maybe, but . . . see, we were back at the hospital," Alexis began. She told them about Atticus waking up, and Camula's Shadow Charm.

"If we can stop her stealing souls, we can duel her with all our might," she explained. "Rather than just standing there scared."

Chazz snorted. "Doesn't scare me."

"Speak for yourself!" the Crowler doll piped up.

"So we fight fire with fire," Alexis continued. "We've got our own Shadow Charm!"

Jaden held out the two halves of the medallion that he wore around his neck. "Compliments of Atticus!"

Atticus had given Jaden his medallion, and the two halves completed the Shadow Charm. Jaden couldn't explain it, but just wearing the charm made him feel stronger.

Jaden led the way to Camula's castle. Once again, they walked up the dark staircase, through the hallway, and into the ballroom. Camula stood on the far balcony, ready for them.

"All right, Camula, let's go!" Jaden cried. "I'm here for my friends' souls! And I'm not leaving till I get them!"

Camilla just smiled. "Actually, truth be told, dear, you're not leaving here ever again," she said. "Not a single one of you is!"

• CHAPTER FOURTEEN •

ILLUSION GATE OPENS AGAIN

Jaden climbed to the opposite balcony and turned on his Duel Disk.

"All right, Camula, get your game on!" he yelled. "'Cause when someone duels my pals and turns their souls into dolls, it puts me in a bad mood!"

"And let me tell *you* something," Camula called back. "I don't care!"

She laughed and activated her Duel Disk. They each drew five cards, and started the duel with 4000 life points each.

"Maybe this will change your mind," Jaden replied. He took one card from his hand and held it up. "Polymerization! I fuse Elemental Heroes Avian, Sparkman, and Bubbleman!"

Jaden had crafted his deck so that it contained hero-type monsters, tall, shining figures with different kinds of powers. His

Polymerization card let him take three heroes and turn them into one larger, more powerful one.

As Jaden held out the cards, Avian, Sparkman, and Bubbleman appeared on the field. They burned with bright light, then swirled in the air. When the light faded, a tall hero stood in front of Jaden. He wore blue armor on his chest and legs, and silver armor on his shoulders. A silver mask covered his face, and large wings grew from his back. The hero had 2800 attack points.

"Introducing Elemental Hero Tempest!" Jaden said proudly.

"Wow! What a way to start the duel!" Syrus said from the floor.

Bastion nodded. "Jaden wants to end this quickly, and with Tempest out there, he might just be able to do it."

"I wouldn't count Camula out just yet," Chazz said.

Professor Banner shivered. "Yes, after all, we've seen how strong her cards can be, especially that Illusion Gate."

Alexis frowned. "We'll just have to hope she doesn't get a chance to play it."

On the balcony, Jaden finished his turn. "Last, I'll throw down a facedown. Let's see what you got!"

"Well, well. If you're in such a hurry to lose, all right," Camula said, smirking. "I play Illusion Gate!"

As Camula played the card, the carved stone gate rose up behind her. Jaden shuddered.

"It had to be *that* one," he muttered.

"I'm sure you remember its effects," the vampire said, clearly enjoying herself. "To begin, all monsters on the field are instantly destroyed. Then I get to summon any monster you've played!"

Camula touched the gold necklace around her throat. The red jewel in the center began to shine. Jaden realized — it must be her Shadow Charm!

"And all I need to pay for all of this is a soul to the Sacred Beasts should I happen to lose this duel." She hungrily eyed the duelists below her. "Now, who's going to be the lucky one?"

The doors of the gate swung open. A foul-smelling black mist floated out of the doors, then reached out to touch Jaden's friends like long fingers. The friends choked and coughed from the stench.

"Oh, dear me, this decision is just too hard to make," Camula said. "Why don't I just put all your friends at stake?"

"What? All of them?" Jaden asked.

"Never underestimate the power of the Shadow," Camula said boldly. "With this necklace, I can do anything!"

Suddenly, the two halves of the medallion that Jaden wore began to glow and shake. The pieces joined together to form a circle.

A beam of pure, cleansing white light poured from Jaden's Shadow Charm. The white light pushed back the black mist, then slammed into Camula up on the balcony. She wailed and reached out, trying to keep her balance.

The doors of Illusion Gate slammed shut.

"What happened?" Chazz wondered.

"Jaden's Shadow Charm canceled the power of her necklace," Alexis explained.

Camula let out a howl of anger. Her eyes flashed with fire.

"Thanks, Atticus," Jaden said under his breath. Then he stared down Camula. "Looks like if you still want to use Illusion Gate, you have to do some soul searching without my friends!

So whadya say you put away that cheating card and get on with this duel!"

"I think not!" Camula shot back. She held out her arms. "Illusion Gate! Open your doors and accept *my* soul as the sacrifice!"

◆ CHAPTER FIFTEEN ◆

VAMPIRE WEREWOLF RETURNS

A bright purple light flashed from the doors of Illusion Gate. The light beams raced across the field and slammed into Tempest. The hero shattered into a million pieces.

"Tempest!" Jaden cried.

"Don't worry, you'll see him again soon," Camula said. "But he'll be fighting for me!"

As soon as she said the words, Elemental Hero Tempest appeared next to Camula. Jaden cringed to see one of his best Duel Monsters in the clutches of the vampire.

"Next, I summon Zombie Werewolf in attack mode!" Camula cried.

The muscled, furry beast appeared, with 1200 attack points next to him.

Camula's eyes narrowed. "Now, Elemental Hero Tempest, attack Jaden!"

The hero had no choice. He aimed the barrel-shaped weapon on the end of his right arm across the ballroom. A tunnel of blue light exploded from the barrel, slamming into Jaden, who groaned as his life points dropped down to 1200.

"And I'm not done yet," Camula promised. "Zombie Werewolf, atta —"

But the sound of groans from Tempest stopped her.

"Tempest, what is wrong?" she asked.

Across the room, Jaden smirked. "Guess he doesn't like his new boss! But you can forget the two weeks' notice. I think I'll just play my trap Cross Heart! That puts Tempest back on my side."

Jaden turned over the card, and Tempest flew across the room and stood next to Jaden once more. Behind Camula, Illusion Gate faded away.

"Go ahead and take him back!" Camula spat out. "I will still win!"

On the floor, Chumley was impressed. "Looks like Jaden's learned a few new tricks."

"I hope so," the Crowler doll chirped.

With Tempest back on his side, Jaden was able to use him. "Time to teach that werewolf pooch a few new tricks — like how to play dead!" he joked.

Tempest nodded and blasted Zombie Werewolf with blue light. The monster screamed and then vanished from the field. Camula shielded herself with her arms as the attack hit her directly. Her life points dropped to 2400.

Camula cringed for a moment, then stood tall once again.

"How quickly you forget," she taunted Jaden. "When you destroy my werewolf, another one comes from my deck with a little surprise . . . 500 more attack points!"

A howl bounced off the walls of the ballroom as another Zombie Werewolf appeared — but this one had 1700 attack points.

Jaden shrugged. "Maybe a facedown will tame him," he said, placing a card on his Duel Disk.

Camula snarled, annoyed. "Fool! You have much more to worry about than just him. This next turn should prove that."

The vampire held up a card. "I play the spell Pot of Greed! Now I may draw two more cards."

She took two cards from her disk and put them in her hand. She giggled. "Jaden, do you know the only thing worse than a vampire mistress? It's a vampire mistress with a grudge!"

Camula pointed to Zombie Werewolf. "Good-bye, my werewolf," she said. "I sacrifice you to summon Vampire Lord!"

The werewolf flashed off the field, and a tall Vampire Lord took its place. Jaden had a sinking feeling he knew what was coming next. He had seen Camula make this move before.

"And now I'll remove Vampire Lord from play to summon Vampire Genesis!" Camula cried.

Her most powerful monster appeared in Vampire Lord's place, his 3000 attack points flashing next to him. Jaden had seen Vampire Genesis before, and it looked just as scary every time.

Camula held up another card. "Next I'll use the spell card Genesis Crisis," she said. "Now, on every turn, a zombie-type monster is transferred directly from my deck into my hand! And with Vampire Genesis, I can discard that monster to the graveyard to summon another one. It can be any zombie monster, as long as it is a lower level."

Jaden frowned. Basically, the cards were giving Camula the ability to create an unending army of zombie monsters.

"So I'll be discarding my Ryu Kokki to bring back vamp's best friend: Zombie Werewolf!" Camula announced.

The resurrected werewolf appeared next to Camula again, although now it was back down to 1200 attack points.

And Camula still wasn't finished. "Now, if I recall, your Elemental Hero cannot be destroyed in battle as long as you sacrifice one of the other cards on your field," she said.

Jaden gasped. How did she know his cards so well?

"And it seems you have one," she continued, eyeing his facedown card. "Pity if something should happen to it, like, for example, if it disappeared due to my Giant Trunade!"

Camula held up a card with a green monsterlike face swirling in green wind. She played the card, and the wind whipped out, wiping Jaden's card off the playing field.

"How'd she know to do that?" Syrus wondered.

"I don't know," Bastion replied. "Camula knows our decks better than anyone. And what's more, she's calculated a perfect strategy against them!"

"So isn't the villain supposed to tell the charming hero how she did it?" Jaden asked. "'Cause I'm all ears!"

Camula's eyes glowed with bloodred fire. "You didn't think my bats were just for decoration, did you? They were spying on each and every one of you!"

A few bats flew up to Camula, flapping their wings rapidly.

"And just as they told me the weaknesses of your pathetic little friends, Crowler and Zane, they told me yours!" Camula cried. "You can't win!"

76

CHAPTER SIXTEEN

A NEW HERO RISES

"And now, Vampire Genesis, attack that Tempest!" Camula commanded. "Crimson Storm!"

A bloodred wind whipped around Vampire Genesis's body. The wind carried Genesis across the ballroom and pummeled Tempest. The hero cried out, then exploded into the red wind. Vampire Genesis appeared next to Camula again.

Jaden's friends watched, worried, from the floor.

"So much for that Elemental Hero Tempest," Chazz said. "Now Jaden's out there like a sitting duck!"

"And I think Zombie Werewolf likes duck," Syrus said nervously. Jaden had only 1200 life points — exactly the same as the werewolf's attack points. "This could be it, guys!"

"This is very anti-licious!" Chumley wailed.

"Zombie Werewolf, attack Jaden directly!" Camula cried.

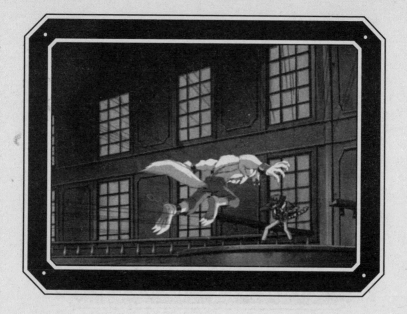

Zombie Werewolf sprang across the ballroom in one motion, growling and snarling. It scratched Jaden with its sharp claws. Jaden lowered his head to protect himself from the attack — but he didn't fall.

"Fall down!" Camula screamed. "You should have no more life points left!"

Jaden raised his head — and he was laughing.

"Guess again, Camula," he said.

"How is this?" the vampire asked, stunned.

"*Insurance* is how," Jaden replied. "When you sent my facedown card, Insurance, back to my hand, its effect went off. I got 500 life points just in time!"

That meant Jaden was still holding on, with 300 life points left.

"I see," Camula said, calm once again. "How fortunate for you. But you just postpone the inevitable. I activate the magic of Genesis Crisis! And now I'll add another zombie monster from my deck to my hand."

Jaden groaned as Camula gained another card. His friends weren't happy, either.

"Jaden's hanging on, but still, Camula has way more life points than him," Alexis pointed out.

"For sure," Chumley agreed. "Shadow Charm or not, how could we let him duel Camula? He's just not at the top of his game. We might as well hand over the spirit keys right now."

"There's always hope," Bastion said, trying to stay positive. "But I admit, with that Vampire Genesis *and* that Genesis Crisis on the field, there isn't much of it."

Professor Banner nervously stroked Pharaoh. "Let's bargain with her — maybe put her in touch with the local blood bank?"

Jaden looked down at his friends. "I think this is bigger than that, Professor. I mean, sure vampires crave blood, but I think *this one* craves our spirit keys a lot more!"

Camula's pale eyes narrowed. "Pathetic mortal," she sneered. "You have no idea what I crave. Centuries ago, the vampires were a proud and peaceful race. We lived in harmony with our mortal brothers and sisters. That is, until the dark times . . . until the war . . ."

A sad look crossed Camula's face as she told her story.

"No one knew who struck first," she went on. "But the fighting was fierce. Neither soldier nor child was spared the horror as hatred decimated both our peoples."

Camula's voice wavered. "I, the last of my race, had no choice but to go into hiding. For years I slept, a coffin as my home. Then a stranger approached. The dark power of Shadow

coursed through his veins. He offered me a choice: Spend an eternity in my tomb or accept his Shadow Charm and join his quest for the Sacred Beast cards. For each duelist that I would beat in battle, a soul would be mine! Which I would use to resurrect my defeated army of vampires, and we would suck our revenge from the bloated vein of humanity!"

Jaden smirked. "Wow, a little too much information there. So if I go down right now, you'll get my key and my soul to start a vampire army?"

The confident look returned to Camula. "You're smart for a mortal. Perhaps you'll do us both a favor and just give up, Jaden. I will make it painless."

"Lady, if you think I'm gonna give up," Jaden said, shaking his head, "you really have gone batty!"

Jaden looked at the cards in his hand. "So here goes . . . something!"

He held up a card. A huge pot with a grinning green face appeared on the field.

"Sweet! I'm starting with Pot of Greed — or in this case, pot of need," Jaden joked, "'cause that's what I've got."

Jaden took two more cards from his deck. He played one right away.

"I play Dark Factory of Mass Production!" he cried. "That lets me take two monsters from the graveyard and put them right back in my hand!"

Jaden pulled two heroes from his graveyard — Sparkman and Avian. He studied his cards. He had another hero in his hand already — Burstinatrix. And one more card that would help turn the tide in this duel . . .

"Now I activate Fusion Gate!" Jaden said with excitement in his voice. "You can forget about Polymerization. This baby lets me fusion summon without it!"

"So what?" Camula asked.

"So check out Avian and Burstinatrix," he called back, holding up the two cards. "Or should I say Elemental Hero Flame Wingman!"

A brightly colored hero appeared in place of the two heroes. Wingman had red and green armor. Bright flames decorated his black mask. One of his arms ended in a red dragon's head, and the other side of its body had a powerful wing.

But Jaden had more tricks up his sleeve.

"There's more!" he announced. "I'm fusing Wingman and the Sparkman in my hand to make something even better."

Jaden's friends gasped. They hadn't seen a move like this before.

"Two fusions?" Alexis wondered.

Sparkman's blue and gold body merged with Wingman, and a new hero appeared in a flash of blinding light. Shining Flare Wingman's armor was made of pure silver that shined as brightly as the sun. Its flowing silver wings made the hero look almost angelic.

Its 2500 attack points flashed next to the hero. Camula grimaced and tried to shield her pale face from the light.

Jaden grinned. "All right, Flare Wingman. Let's get our pals' souls back!"

‹ CHAPTER SEVENTEEN ›

SOLAR FLARE!

"Flare Wingman! You've never used that card in your deck before!" Camula sounded like a disappointed child. Then her tone changed to an angry growl. "You have to be cheating. You put it in there when I wasn't looking, didn't you?"

"Uh, yeah," Jaden replied. "But I'm not so sure that's cheating. I mean, you were the one spying! And anyway, I didn't sneak it in."

"You lie!" Camula growled.

"Nah, not really," Jaden said, scratching his head. "I just figured since you were all about the shadows, I should pack something that's bright — like Elemental Hero Shining Flare Wingman. And boy, is he! Check out that glow!"

"Fine," Camula sneered. "Use him. With just 2500 points, he still won't defeat Vampire Genesis!"

Jaden grinned. "Actually, Camula, yeah, he will. 'Cause for each of my Elemental Heroes that are just chillin' away back at the graveyard, Flare Wingman gains 300 attack points!"

Jaden had two Elemental Heroes in the graveyard — Bubbleman and Tempest. That added 600 points to Flare Wingman's attack, bringing it to 3100 — 100 more than Vampire Genesis.

The realization dawned on Camula. "Then my vampire . . ."

"Is about to bite the dust!" Jaden finished for her. "Shining Flare Wingman, show this lady how we do things back at Duel Academy. Attack Vampire Genesis with Solar Flare!"

Shining Flare Wingman let out a heart-pumping battle cry

as it flew across the ballroom. A white-hot solar flare erupted from its body, hurling toward Vampire Genesis.

The solar beam engulfed Vampire Genesis. The beast's body exploded in a blaze of burning white light and heat. Camula took the remaining damage, and her life points dropped to 2300.

"And when Vampire Genesis is not on the field, all zombie-type monsters you have out are destroyed!" Jaden cried gleefully.

Camula screamed in anger as her Zombie Werewolf burst apart. Then she glared at Jaden.

"Sorry, but it takes more than that to defeat a vampire," she said.

"Good, 'cause I got more for you," Jaden replied. "Flare Wingman's special ability! And it's better than a wooden stake. You get hit for damage equal to the attack points of the monster I just destroyed!"

A look of terror captured Camula's face. "No! It can't be!"

But Jaden was right. Another white light erupted in front of Camula. She screamed and then fell to her knees. Her life points dropped to zero.

At that moment, the Illusion Gate arose once again behind Camula. She had vowed to sacrifice her soul to the Sacred Beasts if she lost the battle — and her time had come. The gate's heavy gray doors opened. A white mist floated out, a mist so cold it chilled the entire ballroom.

Camula turned toward the gate to face her fate. The mist took the shape of a claw. It reached out and grabbed Camula, pulling a purple mist from her body — her soul. Camula collapsed. Then her body slowly vanished.

As the doors to the gate shut, two of Camula's posses-

sions clattered to the floor: the cloth doll that held Zane's soul, and her Shadow Charm, the gold necklace.

"That's game!" Jaden cried, pumping his fist in the air.

Syrus ran up to the balcony, toward his brother's doll. As he ran, the doll transformed back into his brother. Zane lay on the balcony, still, with his eyes closed.

"Big bro!" Syrus cried.

At the same time, Crowler's doll transformed into the professor — while he was still in Chazz's pocket. He clung to Chazz.

"I'm back!" he cried. "Now get me out of this stinking pocket!"

"What, now it's not good enough for you?" Chazz snapped. "Next time, I'll leave you in a dollhouse with a toy car and a plastic wife!"

But the friends didn't have time to celebrate.

"Jaden, the castle is falling apart!" Alexis warned. She pointed at the stone walls, which were beginning to shake and crumble.

"Let's go!" Bastion yelled.

Chumley and Syrus helped Zane, and they all charged out of the castle as fast as they could. They didn't look back until they had crossed the red-carpet bridge and reached the shore of the lake.

The morning sun was rising over the horizon as they turned to look at the castle. The structure collapsed in a shower of stone and dust.

Bastion handed Jaden Camula's necklace, the Shadow Charm she had used to steal souls. Jaden studied it.

"This nightmare's over," he said. "But Camula was just the

second of the Shadow Riders. And that means . . . more are on the way."

  Jaden looked up at the rising sun. Whatever waited for him around the corner, he was ready . . . ready to get his game on again!